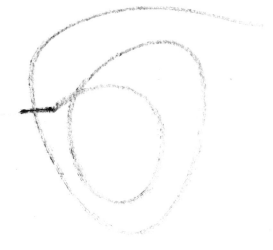

The Three Bears

DEAR CAREGIVER, The *Beginning-to-Read* series is a carefully written collection of classic readers you may remember from your own childhood. Each book features text comprised of common sight words to provide your child ample practice reading the words that appear most frequently in written text. The many additional details in the pictures enhance the story and offer the opportunity for you to help your child expand oral language and develop comprehension.

Begin by reading the story to your child, followed by letting him or her read familiar words and soon your child will be able to read the story independently. At each step of the way, be sure to praise your reader's efforts to build his or her confidence as an independent reader. Discuss the pictures and encourage your child to make connections between the story and his or her own life. At the end of the story, you will find reading activities and a word list that will help your child practice and strengthen beginning reading skills.

Above all, the most important part of the reading experience is to have fun and enjoy it!

Shannon Cannon

Shannon Cannon,
Literacy Consultant

Norwood House Press • P.O. Box 316598 • Chicago, Illinois 60631
For more information about Norwood House Press please visit our website at
www.norwoodhousepress.com or call 866-565-2900.

LIBRARY OF CONGRESS CATALOGING-IN-PUBLICATION DATA

Hillert, Margaret.
The three bears / by Margaret Hillert ; illustrated by Irma Wilde.— Rev. and expanded library ed.
p. cm. — (Beginning to read series. Fairy tales and folklore)
Summary: Lost in the woods, a tired and hungry little girl finds the home of the three bears where she helps herself to food and goes to sleep.
ISBN-13: 978-1-59953-026-0 (library edition : alk. paper)
ISBN-10: 1-59953-026-0 (library edition : alk. paper)
[1. Folklore. 2. Bears—Folklore.] I. Wilde, Irma, ill. II. Title. III. Series.

2005033533

The Three Bears

by Margaret Hillert

Illustrated by Irma Wilde

NORWOODHOUSE PRESS

See the house.
It is red and yellow.
It is a funny little house.

One, two, three.
One is the father.
One is the mother.
One is the baby.

The father is big.
The baby is little.

See Mother work.
Mother can make something.

Away we go.
Away, away, away.

I can play.
My ball is blue.
See it go up.

Oh, look.
Here is a little house.
A funny little house.
I can go in.

Here is something.
Red, yellow, and blue.
One is big.
One is little.

I want something.
Here is one for me.

Here is something.
Red, yellow, and blue.
One is big.
One is little.

Here is one for me.

Here is something.
Red, yellow, and blue.
One is big.
One is little.

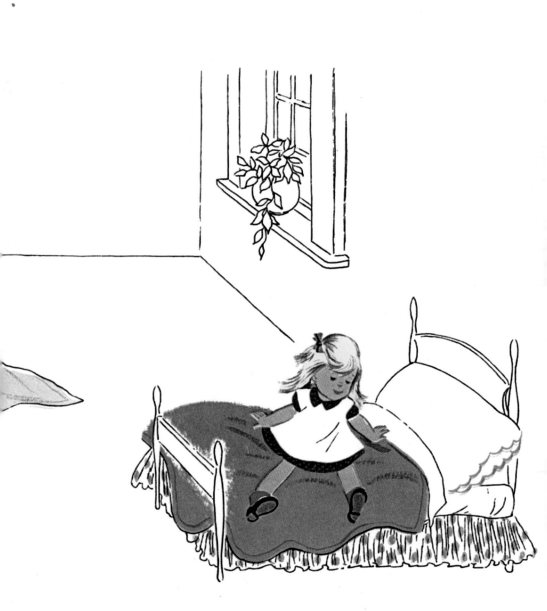

Here is one for me.

Here we come.

We can go in.

Father said, "Oh, oh!"
Mother said, "Oh, my!"
Baby said, "Oh, look!
It is not here."

Father said, "Oh, oh!"
Mother said, "Oh, my!"
Baby said, "Oh, look!
It is down."

Father said, "Oh, oh!"
Mother said, "Oh, my!"
Baby said, "Oh, look!
I see something."

Help, help!
I can jump down.
I can run.

Oh, Mother, Mother.

Here I come!

READING REINFORCEMENT

The following activities support the findings of the National Reading Panel that determined the most effective components for reading instruction are: Phonemic Awareness, Phonics, Vocabulary, Fluency, and Text Comprehension.

Phonemic Awareness: The /s/ sound

Oddity Task: Say the /s/ sound for your child. Say the following words aloud. Ask your child to say the word that does not end with the /s/ sound in the following word groups:

bus, yes, yet	gas, gab, kiss	cab, bats, cabs	miss, mess, mix
us, play, plus	this, less, fast	set, loss, toss	past, pass, pats

Phonics: The letter Ss

1. Demonstrate how to form the letters **S** and **s** for your child.
2. Have your child practice writing **S** and **s** at least three times each.
3. Ask your child to point to the words in the book that start with the letter **s**.
4. Write down the following words and ask your child to circle the letter **s** in each word:

see	sit	is	Sam	say	was
saw	bears	sat	kiss	something	she
basket	pass	star	said	house	sun

Vocabulary: Number Words

1. Explain to your child that numbers can be written as words or numerals.

2. Write the following words on separate pieces of paper:

zero   one   two   three   four   five

six   seven   eight   nine   ten

3. Read each word to your child and ask your child to repeat it.

4. Mix the words up. Point to a word and ask your child to read it. Provide clues if your child needs them.

5. Hold up any number of fingers from zero to ten and ask your child to point to the correct word that represents that number.

6. Write the numbers 0–10 on separate pieces of paper and ask your child to match the numerals with the number words.

7. When your child has mastered these first numbers, you may wish to repeat the activity again for numbers eleven to twenty.

Fluency: Shared Reading

1. Reread the story to your child at least two more times while your child tracks the print by running a finger under the words as they are read. Ask your child to read the words he or she knows with you.

2. Reread the story taking turns, alternating readers between sentences or pages.

Text Comprehension: Discussion Time

1. Ask your child to retell the sequence of events in the story.

2. To check comprehension, ask your child the following questions:

• Who are the members of the bear family?

• What was the little girl doing when the bears came home?

• How do you think the bears felt when they came home?

• Who are the people in your family?

WORD LIST

The Three Bears uses the 45 words listed below.

This list can be used to practice reading the words that appear in the text. You may wish to write the words on index cards and use them to help your child build automatic word recognition. Regular practice with these words will enhance your child's fluency in reading connected text.

a	go	make	said
and		me	see
away	help	mother	something
	here	my	
baby	house		the
ball		not	three
big	I		two
blue	in	oh	
	is	one	up
can	it		
come		play	want
	jump		we
down		red	work
	little	run	
father	look		yellow
for			
funny			

ABOUT THE AUTHOR Margaret Hillert has written over 80 books for children who are just learning to read. Her books have been translated into many different languages and over a million children throughout the world have read her books. She first started writing poetry as a child and has continued to write for children and adults throughout her life. A first grade teacher for 34 years, Margaret is now retired from teaching and lives in Michigan where she likes to write, take walks in the morning, and care for her three cats.

Photograph by Glenna Washburn

ABOUT THE ADVISER Shannon Cannon contributed the activities pages that appear in this book. Shannon serves as a literacy consultant and provides staff development to help improve reading instruction. She is a frequent presenter at educational conferences and workshops. Prior to this she worked as an elementary school teacher and as president of a curriculum publishing company.